SHAWN and KEEPER
and the Birthday Party

by Jonathan London
illustrated by Renée Williams-Andriani

Dutton Children's Books • New York

For Sean and Keeper, and Skeena too—J.L.
For Maggie, Ellen, and Joseph—R.W.-A.

Text copyright © 1999 by Jonathan London
Illustrations copyright © 1999 by Renée Williams-Andriani
All rights reserved.

CIP data is available.

Published in the United States 1999 by Dutton Children's Books,
a division of Penguin Putnam Books for Young Readers
345 Hudson Street, New York, New York 10014
http://www.penguinputnam.com/yreaders/index.htm

Printed in Hong Kong
First Edition

3 5 7 9 10 8 6 4

ISBN 0-525-46115-9

Shawn and Keeper

were born on the same day.

They grew up together.

When Shawn was a baby,

Keeper was a puppy.

When Shawn turned one,

Keeper turned one too.

Now Shawn was going to be six.

And so was Keeper.

Tomorrow was the big day!

Keeper helped Shawn choose a cake.

"Strawberry!" Shawn told Mom.

"Woof!" barked Keeper.

Keeper helped Shawn

pick a piñata for the party.

"A pig or a dog?" asked Shawn.

"Woof!" barked Keeper.

"A dog it is," said Shawn.

Keeper helped Shawn

blow up balloons.

"Pop!" went every balloon

that Keeper tried to catch.

That night, Shawn lay awake.

He was thinking about the party.

Keeper lay awake beside him.

"Oh boy," said Shawn. "I can't wait!"

When Shawn woke up,

he smelled the cake baking.

"Yum!" said Shawn,

and they ran downstairs.

"Can I have a bite?" asked Shawn.

"No cake now!" said Mom.

"Help Dad hang the balloons."

"Can I have a bite?" asked Shawn.

"No cake now!" said Dad.

"Help me hang the piñata."

"Can I have a bite?" asked Shawn.

"No cake now!" said Mom.

"Your friends are here."

And the party began!

Shawn and his friends did the limbo.

So did Keeper.

They played pin the tail on the donkey.

Keeper played too.

Shawn and his friends

hit the piñata.

Keeper ran and hid.

They had hot dogs, chips, and drinks.

Then Shawn yelled, "The cake! The cake!

It's time for the cake!"

"Oh no!" Mom shouted.

"The cake is gone!"

She held up an empty cake pan.

"Keeper!" shouted Shawn.

Shawn and his friends went hunting
for Keeper and the cake.
They looked in the kitchen.

They looked in the bathroom.

They looked in the yard.

"Keeper!" shouted Shawn.

Keeper came over.

He looked sheepish.

"Where's my cake?" asked Shawn.

"Here it is!" said Dad.

"Surprise!"

He had added Keeper's name to the cake.

"Hurray!" everybody shouted.

Shawn gave Keeper a hug.

Together, Shawn and Keeper
blew out the candles.
"Did you make a wish, Keeper?"
asked Shawn.
"Woof!" barked Keeper.

Keeper got his wish.

He got a chunk of cake.

"Happy birthday!" sang Shawn.

"Woof!" barked Keeper.

And when they tore open their presents,

they howled with joy.